THE KISS OF DEATH

A SHORT STORY

ALEXANDRIA BLAELOCK

BlueMere Books
MELBOURNE, AUSTRALIA

For permission requests, please contact
enquiries@bluemerebooks.com.

Ordering Information:
Discounts are available on quantity purchases. For details, contact orders@bluemerebooks.com.

The Kiss of Death/Alexandria Blaelock
paperback ISBN: 978-0-6481733-1-1
digital ISBN: 978-0-6481733-2-8

Book Layout © BookDesignTemplates.com

BlueMere Books
www.bluemerebooks.com

THE KISS OF DEATH

I don't remember the first time I saw Him.
Which now that I think about it, is kind of strange.

Despite His striking looks, my eyes couldn't seem to find any purchase on His face and just slid straight off.

The first time I do remember seeing Him, I was frowning into space, trying to work out my share of the restaurant bill.

And all of a sudden, there He was.

Sitting alone. On a worn black leather seat, in a dimly lit booth across the room. Looking at me.

Elbows resting on the wood table, holding half a glass of red wine in both hands, watching over the rim.

With His pale face and shock of dark hair, He was repellent, yet fascinating.

There was a silence between us, that put the usual restaurant sounds of conversation and cutlery clattering on plates on mute.

You know what it's like when you suddenly realise you're staring at someone and making them uncomfortable?

We locked eyes for a moment before I flushed with embarrassment and looked away.

And when I looked back, as you always do, He was gone.

Nowhere to be seen.

No empty wine glass, or any other kind of indication He had been there.

But having seen Him once, it seemed He couldn't or didn't want to hide from me, and I'd sometimes catch glimpses of Him here and there.

You know how sometimes you get the feeling that someone's behind you?

And you turn quickly, hoping to catch them in the act. But there's no one there.

Yet you feel a lingering presence you can't explain.

That's how it was with Him.

Sometimes I caught sight of a dark blur, and sometimes there was just a hole in the space, as though someone had pushed the emergency exit button.

It made me feel odd - a strange combination of excited butterflies and sick to my stomach.

Something momentous was happening, and I didn't know if it was good or bad. Like someone was walking over my grave.

I started to notice that no one else saw Him.

Crowds parted to walk around Him but didn't seem to notice they weren't walking straight and true. Each time I saw Him, he was a little closer, and I couldn't look away.

I was exhilarated and terrified.

Sometimes, when I bought my morning latte, I'd think I saw Him across the cafe.

Or when I was browsing a shop, the hair on the back of my neck would stand on end, and I'd turn and catch a glimpse of Him walking away.

One day, I saw Him merging back into the crowd, and I'd had enough.

All that exchanging glances across a crowded room was just ridiculous. I thought I was too old for that nonsense; it was time to make contact.

I wanted to know just what the hell He thought He was playing at.

And when I thought about it, I remembered the only times He hadn't disappeared were when we'd made eye contact.

So, the next time I saw Him, I was talking to a friend in a crowded evening street.

We were supposed to be having a meal together, but when I caught His eye, I left her without a second glance and started walking towards Him.

This time He waited.

I didn't blink, I didn't look away, I didn't give Him the opportunity to disappear.

Or maybe He didn't want to.

But whatever the reason, He waited as I approached.

I didn't quite know what to do when I reached Him.

A dozen half-formed sentences died on my parted lips as I looked at up Him. He looked back, a small smile lifting one corner of His mouth.

Then someone bumped me, and He was gone.

I turned to look for Him, then spun again and again, but He was gone.

We'd been so close we'd almost touched.

Even in that short a time, I felt He'd seen into the depths of my soul.

Not like your friends who're too busy checking their phones or thinking about what they're going to say next to look at you.

No one seems to look long enough to really see you anymore.

It went on like that again that for weeks, seeing Him on and off.

Sometimes it seemed I had only the vaguest dreamlike memories of Him. Not only could I not see Him, but I couldn't remember Him either.

But whether it was weeks or months or years, I saw Him again.

I was late for work and having just picked up my latte from my usual overcrowded cafe on the way. I was juggling coffee, wallet and phone earbuds, still sounding tinny music.

When I turned, I almost walked straight into His outstretched arm.

You know, like when someone is reaching out their hand to touch your shoulder, or brush a stray lock of hair from your face.

"Oh," I said, "I didn't see there."

He smiled His lopsided smile, and His fingers lightly brushed my cheek as He started pulling back His hand.

"I didn't want you to," He replied.

His voice was deep and resonant, and I felt its echo, strangely calming and comfortable in my ribcage.

I had no idea what He meant, but maintaining eye contact, I shoved my wallet and headset into my coat pocket and grabbed His hand before he could melt back into the crowd and disappear.

There was no way I was letting Him get away from me again.

His hand was cool and soft to the touch, with short, clean fingernails.

A small shiver ran down His arm, as though He wasn't used to being touched.

Or the heat of my latte warmed hand had burnt Him.

Yet He did not pull His hand away.

In fact, He slipped his fingers between mine and pulled me closer. So close, our bodies lightly touched.

And still, He held my eyes looking down at me with a combination of sardonic humour, distaste and hope.

I couldn't breathe, couldn't move away, or move closer.

He took a step back as if testing to see if I'd follow.

Then another and another, and within very few steps we weren't in the cafe anymore. We were somewhere else.

At odds with our arrival, it was a perfectly ordinary, if spartan sitting room.

Dark leather sofas surrounded a low table stacked with books. A pair of shoes lay haphazardly nearby on the pale wooden floor as if He'd toed them off and kicked them out of the way before falling back onto the sofa and reaching for a book.

The window overlooked a bleak, grey-toned landscape, and the light streaming in gave no indication whether it was morning or evening.

The room was neither warm nor cool, and dust motes floated lazily in the air. It smelled like a cold fire you'd tried unsuccessfully to rekindle.

The only sound was my breathing. Maybe a little faster and shallower than normal.

There was nothing untoward, yet my skin prickled, and my heart pounded so hard in my chest, I thought it might burst from my body.

As I stood looking up at Him, I finally understood that despite appearances, He wasn't an ordinary man.

He had a restful coolness and a stillness about Him that made my fears and worries seem irrelevant.

There was a sort of small something nagging at the edge of my mind, but when He dipped His head, and His cold lips finally met mine, time stood still.

And I didn't care what it was.

I was not one of those people who think they're special.

I never thought I was made for anything greater.

I didn't expect to do or be anything extraordinary

But at that moment, I knew He was the half of me that had been missing since before I was born.

That just as winter follows summer and day ends at night, so life ends at death and oh my god!

Death is a good kisser.

As His still cool arms surrounded me, I thought I might burst into flames so hot they would consume us both for all eternity.

And as one of His hands slid beneath my shirt...

Well, I dropped my latte and reached out for him.

The sound of my coffee hitting the floor startled us apart, and we stood panting, not meeting each other's eyes.

It took all my courage to look up at Him.

He had turned away and was looking out the window, but somehow, I could see through His aloofness to the yearning below.

To this day, I don't know what made me so bold.

Maybe it was His loneliness and hunger for connection.

Or my selfish desire to be the centre of attention.

Just once.

But whatever the reason, I dropped my bag, slipped off my coat and kicked off my shoes.

He looked over His shoulder at me, and as our eyes met, I started unbuttoning my blouse.

That was all it took.

He reached for me, kissing my throat as His hands pushed my blouse from my shoulders. I felt my knees buckle and fell back onto a sofa pulling Him with me.

I grabbed His shirt, and as it parted from His jeans, it tore open.

He pulled back slowly as each button fell to the ground with a plink.

His dark eyes were unreadable.

I thought maybe I'd offended Him, but I was enveloped by the scent of warm earth after a thunderstorm and didn't care.

I just wanted Him.

I reached for His belt, and that seemed enough. A frenzied flurry of pulling and tugging, and I was gasping as He sank into me.

But as it turns out, I should have read the fine print because once you take the hand of Death, there's no going back.

And being Death's lover has its disadvantages.

Don't get me wrong, I love Him, and I know He loves me.

And I'm not sure that even knowing the price I would've turned him down.

Leaving Him in Spring is torture, and I count the days until Autumn when I can return home.

Though some days, I wonder if I miss the dog more than Him.

I used to worry he had a Northern Hemisphere Lover too, but I've never seen any evidence of her.

Maybe He has another residence up there, though I don't know why He'd bother.

Death is eternal and unchanging, but I'm not.

I worry that He'll start looking for someone younger and prettier.

Someone people don't think is His mother.

He laughs and tells me not to worry that it's only and always me He looks for, lifetime after lifetime.

Not that it affects His passion for me.

Or that I age when I'm with Him, but when I leave, my clock starts clicking again.

It was harder the first few years; trying to explain to my friends and family where I'd been, why I didn't answer my phone and why my hair was now white.

You can't tell them the truth - you've been in the Underworld, and there's no mobile coverage.

And even if you did, they'd think you were joking.

I can't tell you how hard it was to set up the mail and message forwarding.

As technology changed, it became why I wasn't on Facebook, why wasn't I watching *The Bachelor*, and why I persisted with my remote "job".

Couldn't I take a job somewhere closer with better phone coverage?

Not to mention being set up on an endless round of blind dates.

As if anyone could ever compete with Him.

As if I could ever explain the situation.

It's been nearly 40 years now, and people are wondering why don't look my age.

I'm not sure how much longer the excuses of a stress-free healthy lifestyle and good skincare are going to work.

He's starting to come for my friends and family too.

I'm not sure how much longer I can continue to be with them in my seemingly unchanging state.

Probably not more than another decade or so.

Can you get cosmetic surgery to look older?

Is it time to start thinking about faking my death?

Though who knows where medical technology will end up.

He tells me not to worry about it, but no matter how long we've been together, I am only human.

I wonder a little what's going to happen to me when I'm old and frail. Will I die at home or out here?

Will I spend the last few years of my life in a nursing home?

Will my charming "grandson" visit me?

They say that the only certainties in life are death and taxes, but He's really not that predictable to me.

It seems the longer I know Him, the less I understand Him.

Perhaps they (and Thackeray) are more right when they say "Love makes fools of us all."

THE END

ABOUT THE AUTHOR

Alexandria Blaelock writes stories, some of them for *Ellery Queen's Mystery Magazine* and *Pulphouse Fiction Magazine*. She's also written four self-help books applying business techniques to personal matters like getting dressed, cleaning house, and feeding your friends.

As a recovering Project Manager, she's probably too fond of sticking to plan. She lives in a forest because she enjoys birdsong, the scent of gum leaves and the sun on her face. When not telecommuting to parallel universes from her Melbourne based imagination, she watches K-dramas, talks to animals, and drinks Campari. At the same time.

Discover more at www.alexandriablaelock.com.

OTHER SHORT STORIES BY ALEXANDRIA BLAELOCK

BOOKS BY
ALEXANDRIA BLAELOCK

Stress Free Dinner Parties
Build Your Signature Wardrobe
Holistic Personal Finance
Ms Blaelock's Book of Minimally Viable
Housekeeping